# STORYTIME COLLECTION

## This book belongs to

Harry Nimah

# Autumn
## Publishing

Published in 2020
by Autumn Publishing
Cottage Farm
Sywell
NN6 0BJ
www.igloobooks.com

© 2019 Disney Enterprises, Inc.
Autumn is an imprint of Bonnier Books UK

0920 003
4 6 8 10 9 7 5 3
ISBN 978-1-78905-238-1

Printed and manufactured in China

# Disney
# Bambi

STORYTIME COLLECTION

One beautiful spring morning, an excited rabbit called Thumper had some news that he couldn't wait to share with all his animal friends. They all rushed to a cosy clearing where a mother deer lay with her new baby.

"Hello, little prince!" they called.

The young prince couldn't wait to meet his new friends and tried to stand up on his long, thin legs. As soon as he was up, he fell straight back down again!

"Kinda wobbly, isn't he," Thumper giggled. "Whatcha gonna call him?"

The doe looked tenderly at her baby and smiled.

"I think I'll call him Bambi," she said.

As Bambi grew, he got less and less wobbly and enjoyed exploring the forest with Thumper.

"Those are birds," Thumper explained, as a flock of baby bluebirds nibbled berries on a branch.

"Burr!" said Bambi, trying to copy his friend.

"Say bird," Thumper corrected.

"Bird!" shouted Bambi and all the startled birds scattered into the air.

"Bird!" cried Bambi when a yellow butterfly landed on his tail.

"That's a butterfly," laughed Thumper.

The butterfly flew off towards a patch of brightly coloured flowers and Bambi followed it.

"Butterfly," Bambi said, poking his nose into the beautiful blooms.

"No, Bambi, that's a flower," chuckled Thumper.

Bambi bent down to sniff the beautiful flowers but suddenly found himself nose-to-nose with a new furry friend.

"Flower," said Bambi to the surprised skunk.

Giggling, Thumper tried to correct his friend but the young skunk stopped him.

"Aw, that's OK," said the shy little skunk. "He can call me Flower if he wants to."

Thumper and Bambi carried on playing until a loud crash of thunder echoed across the forest sky and it started to rain.

Back home in a group of trees called a thicket, Bambi
snuggled up close to his mother for a nap. At first, the sound of
the falling rain kept him awake but soon the soft pitter-patter of the
raindrops lulled him to sleep. When the rain finally passed, Bambi's mother
took him on a long walk past a sparkling waterfall. He was excited when she
told him they were going to a beautiful flower-filled meadow.

"Why haven't I been to the meadow before?" Bambi asked her.

"You weren't big enough," she said, hushing him as they reached the edge
of the forest. "We're almost there."

At last, they arrived at the meadow. Bambi was excited to see the endless lush green grass and the bright flowers stretching out in front of him. He immediately wanted to race out and play, but his mother quickly stopped him.

"You must never rush out on the meadow," she scolded. "There might be danger!"

Slowly, she walked out through the trees. When she was certain it was safe, she called Bambi to join her.

Bambi loved playing in the meadow and it didn't seem dangerous to him at all! He had great fun watching a frog hop from rock to rock until it disappeared into a pond with a loud splash.

As Bambi leaned towards the water to look for the frog, he found himself looking at a reflection that was definitely not his!

The reflection Bambi saw in the water belonged to a girl. She smiled and fluttered her eyelashes at Bambi.

"That's little Faline," his mother explained. "Go on," she nudged him. "Say hello."

Bambi closed his eyes and gulped. "Hello," he said.

Faline started a game of tag with Bambi
and soon the pair were leaping and
playing together as if they had
been best friends forever.

Bambi and Faline stopped playing when they heard hooves thundering towards them.

A herd of stags galloped past and one of them – the biggest of all – stopped and looked at Bambi. Feeling nervous, Bambi looked down, but could still feel the stag's majestic gaze upon him.

Later, Bambi asked his mother why everyone was still when the stag arrived at the meadow.

"Everyone respects him," she whispered. "He is very brave and very wise. He is the Great Prince of the Forest."

The silence of the meadow was suddenly shattered by a loud blast. It was a gunshot and it meant Man was nearby. It also meant danger. All the animals were scared and ran from the meadow back to the safety of the forest.

Panicking, Bambi realised he couldn't see his mother and he felt very frightened.

"Bambi! Bambi! Hurry!" He could hear her calling but he still couldn't see her.

Suddenly, the Great Prince was by his side and he guided Bambi safely back to his mother.

Time passed quickly in the forest and there was always something new for Bambi to discover. One morning he woke up to find the forest had turned white!

"It's snow," Bambi's mother told him. "It means winter has come."

Bambi was unsure about the strange white floor that was now covering his home. He trod gently on the snow, it felt wet and cold but he liked the way it crunched under his hooves.

Thumper called Bambi over to the pond, which had frozen solid.

"Watch what I can do!" called Thumper, as he spun and swirled across the ice. "Come on it's all right! The water's stiff."

Bambi watched his friend zooming across the sparkling, icy pond. It looked like fun and he wanted to join in.

"Yippee!" yelled Bambi, as he jumped in the air.
When he landed, all four legs started slipping and sliding in
different directions! With a helpful push from Thumper, Bambi
was soon gliding across the ice.

"Some fun, huh, Bambi?" cried Thumper.

Bambi was skating at last but he still didn't know how to stop! The pair went whizzing across the ice and crashed into a huge pile of snow. In a cave next to where they landed, they found Flower snoring away.

"Wake up, Flower," called Bambi, but the little skunk just yawned and stretched.

"All of us flowers sleep in the winter," Flower said, tucking himself under his tail. "Goodnight."

Winter was fun at first but, after living in the cold for a while, Bambi started to miss the long warm days and the delicious grass and flowers of spring.

"I'm hungry, Mother," Bambi said, as they searched for a few blades of grass buried beneath the snow.

Bambi had never missed the sweet
blossoms from the meadow more.

"Winter seems long, but it won't last
forever," his mother promised him.

At last, Bambi and his mother found
a patch of grass pushing up
through the snow. Bambi
hungrily nibbled on the
grass and it felt
like a feast!

He noticed that his mother wasn't eating and soon he realised why.
She had her head tilted and was listening very carefully.
Then, they both heard that horrible sound again. It was
another gunshot – they were in danger.

"Quick, run for the thicket, Bambi!" his mother instructed.
"Don't look back!"

Bambi ran and ran, his heart pounding as his hooves kicked
up snow behind him.

"Faster!" he heard his mother call. "Keep running!"

Bambi ran as fast as he possibly could and, just as he reached his home, he heard a second gunshot.

"Mother!" Bambi screamed into the snowy woods. "Mother, where are you?"

He frantically searched between the towering trees but she was nowhere to be seen. He listened hard for her voice calling him, but heard only the soft, falling snowflakes and the wind whistling through the bare branches. At that moment, Bambi realised he was all alone.

Bambi was crying when he sensed a tall shadow standing over him. It was the Great Prince and he spoke softly to Bambi.

"Your mother can't be with you any more. Man has taken her away." Bambi lowered his head sadly and swallowed back his tears.

"Come, my son," the stag told him.

Sadly, Bambi looked at his home in the thicket one last time. Then he followed the Great Prince – who he now knew was his father – into the forest.

It wasn't long before springtime once again brought the forest to life. The flowers bloomed, the grass grew, the birds sang and even Flower woke from his long winter nap!

The forest wasn't the only thing changing. Bambi was now a handsome young buck with antlers and Thumper was a fully-grown rabbit.

"Well, well, look how you've grown!" said Friend Owl to the three friends one day. "It won't be long now before you're twitterpated! You get weak in the knees. Your head starts to whirl!" the owl explained

Bambi, Flower and Thumper were puzzled by what he meant.

Bambi and Thumper were certain that they would never allow themselves to be twitterpated.

"It's not gonna happen to me," declared Thumper.

"Me, neither!" agreed Bambi.

Before Flower could agree with them, he met a pretty skunk and fell in love! Shrugging, he waved goodbye to his friends.

"Huh!" Thumper sniffed, disgusted by his friend's behaviour. "Twitterpated!"

Thumper didn't realise that he would be the next one of the friends to be struck by the mysterious condition.

"La, la, la," sang a beautiful bunny. She waved hello with her ear. Then she rubbed noses with Thumper and his foot began thumping.

Bambi also finally understood what twitterpated meant when he saw a familiar reflection in the water as he was drinking from the pond.

"Hello, Bambi!" said a sweet female voice.

Startled, Bambi stumbled back and his antlers got tangled in the nearby branches.

"Don't you remember me?" she said. "I'm Faline." The doe giggled and licked his face.

Bambi suddenly felt dizzy, as if he were light as a feather. He realised this must be what Owl meant!

His dreamy thoughts were interrupted when another stag appeared and challenged him – he wanted to take Faline away from Bambi! The pair locked antlers and tumbled to the ground. Bambi fought fiercely and pushed the stag to the edge of a cliff.

"Bambi!" Faline cried out in fear.

Using all his strength, Bambi butted the stag who rolled down the hill into the river. The stag limped off into the forest, leaving Bambi and Faline to be together.

From that day on, Bambi and Faline were always at each other's side.
They made their home in the thicket and were very happy together.

One day, Bambi yet again sensed danger in the forest.

"It's Man," the Great Prince told him. "There are many this time."

A strong smell of smoke started to drift into the forest and the animals
knew it wouldn't be long before the air was thick with smoke, too.

The crows shouted a warning and fear quickly spread through the forest.

"Be calm! Don't get excited!" urged a pheasant.

It was already too late, the animals feared Man and they panicked!

Thumper gathered his young children and took them to hide in their burrow. Flower and his family went underground. The beavers dived underwater and the squirrels climbed high into the treetops. The other animals raced deeper and deeper into the forest.

"Bambi! Bambi!" Faline cried in terror. She could hear the sounds of Man's angry dogs coming nearer. Barking and biting, they chased her up the rocky cliff, angrily snapping at her heels. She was trapped!

Suddenly, the dogs turned to attack something else.

It was Bambi! He was fighting them off so that Faline could escape. As he charged at the dogs with his sharp antlers, she ran higher up the cliff. Faline was safe but Bambi was still in great danger. Then, a gunshot was fired and he fell to the ground.

He tried as hard as he could but he couldn't get up.

Badly injured, Bambi weakly lifted his head to see smoke pouring through the trees and animals running in fear. Then he heard a familiar voice.

"You must get up!" It was his father, the Great Prince. "Get up!"

Bambi tried again and fell back down. He kept trying and finally staggered to his feet and started to run. Smoke filled the air and the forest was red with flames.

"Follow me," the Great Prince said. "We'll be safe in the river."

The smoke made it hard for Bambi to breathe but his father forced him to carry on to the river. The whole forest was burning around them as they waded into the water. Bambi and his father swam to the waterfalls and, just as a burning tree crashed down behind them, they jumped high in the air and allowed the wall of gushing water to carry them to safety.

When the pair finally reached an island in the river, Faline was waiting for Bambi and she gently licked his wounded shoulder.

That night, the animals watched with horror as fire destroyed their forest home. All the trees and beautiful blossoms were black and destroyed. They were sad but they knew that the fire would soon be gone and they would be able to rebuild their homes.

Sure enough, the forest slowly returned to normal and before long, it was once again spring. New life was appearing everywhere.

"Wake up, Friend Owl!" Thumper cried, as his four baby bunnies all thumped on a hollow log.

"What now?" groaned the grumpy old owl.

The squirrels, pheasants, chipmunks, raccoons and rabbits were all racing towards a familiar thicket.

At the thicket, the animals gazed at Faline and her twin babies.

"Well, sir, I don't believe I've ever seen a more likely lookin' pair of fawns!" the owl said, nodding his head. "Prince Bambi ought to be mighty proud."

Prince Bambi was very proud. He stood with his father on a rock overlooking the thicket where Faline lay with their new fawns. Life was constantly changing in the forest and now he knew that his own life would never be the same again.

Soon, the fawns were ready to start exploring. Bambi, the new Great Prince, was ready to teach them the ways of the forest – just as his father had taught him.

# THE END

# COLLECT THEM ALL!

## With 12 more exciting titles to choose from, you'll want to complete your Storytime Collection!

Can Aladdin and Jasmine stop the evil Jafar?

Will Belle be able to break the curse?

Will Dory finally find her parents?

How far will a father go for his son?

Can Anna and Elsa stop an eternal winter?

Will Mowgli defeat Shere Khan?

Will the Incredibles save the day?

Will Simba ever become king?

Will Ariel be able to find her prince in time?

Can Moana restore the heart of Te Fiti?

Will Maleficent's curse come true?

Will Rapunzel learn who she truly is?